Little Murders

A COMEDY IN TWO ACTS

By Jules Feiffer

SAMUEL FRENCH, INC.

45 WEST 25TH STREET   NEW YORK 10010
7623 SUNSET BOULEVARD   HOLLYWOOD 90046
LONDON   *TORONTO*

ALL RIGHTS RESERVED

ISBN 0 573 61165 3   Printed in U.S.A

CAST OF CHARACTERS

CAROL NEWQUIST, *Patsy's father*

MARJORIE NEWQUIST, *Patsy's mother*

KENNY NEWQUIST, *Patsy's brother*

PATSY NEWQUIST

ALFRED CHAMBERLAIN, *Patsy's fiance*

HENRY DUPAS, *a clergyman*

MILES PRACTICE, *Lieutenant, N.Y.C. Homicide Squad*

THE JUDGE

ASSORTED WEDDING GUESTS

SCENES

The action takes place in the Newquist apartment.

ACT ONE

SCENE 1: An afternoon in February.

SCENE 2: Two months later.

ACT TWO

SCENE 1: Four hours later.

SCENE 2: Six months later.

"2, 4, 6, 8—who do we assassinate?"

New York children's
street chant,
Circa 1964.

Little Murders

ACT ONE

Scene 1

A view of the Newquist *apartment. The living room, dining area, foyer and front door slowly fade into view, [by means of a scrim or any other workable method] in sync with the rising sound of city STREET NOISES. The apartment is typically upper West Side and is clearly tenanted, although at the moment—mid-morning—it is empty. As the apartment fades into view the level of noise rises—morning noise; CONSTRUCTION, TRAFFIC and HELICOPTERS. In the next few minutes both light and noise change: SHADOWS shift, lengthen and darken in sync with the fading of CONSTRUCTION sounds, replaced by the late afternoon cries of CHILDREN at play. Then, this too fades, into the quieter monotone of early evening TRAFFIC. The apartment darkens accordingly and we may even see the sinking SUN as reflected in the apartment windows across the street. [The only view of the outside world is of other buildings, other windows.] What we see is comparable to a stop motion camera's view of the apartment, from mid-morning to dusk. Throughout, a steady patina of SOOT has drifted in through one of the half-open windows—and specks of PLASTER may, now and then, drop from the ceiling. The TELEPHONE rings. Other sounds: POLICE SIRENS, FIRE ENGINES, etc. Front door CHIMES; a pause and then it begins to unlock. This takes time: there are two double locks on the door.*

The door slowly pushes open, revealing two enormous shopping bags. Almost completely hidden behind them is MARJORIE, *small, energetic, in her fifties.*

MARJORIE. Don't let a draft in! (*As she disappears through the swinging door that leads to the kitchen,* KENNY *enters reading a paperback. He is listless, in his early twenties. Leaving the door open he starts slowly across the room, engrossed in his reading. On the return swing of the kitchen door,* MARJORIE *reappears sans coat and shopping bags, this time carrying a folded tablecloth and a large sponge.*) I'm going to need your help, young man. (KENNY *enters bathroom, closes door loudly.*) Don't dawdle! (MARJORIE *runs sponge across dining-room table. It comes up pitch black.*) Filth! (*She unfolds tablecloth in one motion. It falls perfectly into place.*) They'll be here any minute, Kenny!

(*She disappears into kitchen with sponge, reappears on return swing of door with serving cart piled high with dishes and silver. She is about to set table when an explosion of AUTOMOBILE HORNS drives her to window, which she slams shut with great effort. She hastens to other window and switches on AIR CON-DITIONER—a loud hum.* CAROL *enters, carrying brief case. He is a short, thickset, energetic man in his fifties, about* MARJORIE'S *size.*)

CAROL. What the hell is that for? This is February! (*Switches off AIR CONDITIONER.*)

MARJORIE. (*A cheerful but uninterested hug.*) It drowns out the traffic.

CAROL. (*Slips out of embrace.*) All right, when we don't have guests. We don't want people to think we're crazy. Did the liquor come?

MARJORIE. It came. (*Suspicious.*) Why are you so interested in liquor?

CAROL. Don't worry. You've got nothing to worry about.

MARJORIE. You called up twice from the office to ask about the liquor.

CAROL. That's all right. That's perfectly all right. (*Evades her stare.*) You can find out a lot more about somebody, you know, when he's a little— (*Flutters hand to indicate unsteady.*)

MARJORIE. (*Shocked.*) Carol, you're not going to get that poor boy *drunk?*

CAROL. That poor boy wants to marry my Patsy! And don't call me *Carol!*

(*Sound of TOILET FLUSH. KENNY enters from bathroom, reading.*)

MARJORIE. But—dear—you haven't even met him!

KENNY. (*Matter of fact.*) He's an artsy-fartsy photographer. Patsy says he's thirty-six but I know he's forty.

CAROL. (*To KENNY.*) Are you *reading* again? (*Grabs paperback.*) "Harlots of Venus"! Is that what I spend seven thousand a year on Graduate School for? Get dressed!

KENNY. You lost my place. (KENNY *exits.*)

CAROL. Why is she doing this to me?

MARJORIE. He'll be a fine boy. I know it in my bones.

CAROL. What are you talking about? Do you have the slightest idea what you're talking about? She's only known him three weeks! I bet he's a fag!

MARJORIE. Carol!

CAROL. (*Vicious.*) I *hate* that name! I told you never to call me that name. You deliberately do that to annoy me! (*Shouts.*) Call me "Dear"! (*Subsides.*) You refuse to look at the facts. This whole family. That's the trouble with it. I'm the only one who looks at the facts. What was the name of that interior decorator she went to Europe with?

MARJORIE. Howard. He was—delicate.

CAROL. Swish! And that *actor*, the one who she went camping up in Maine with?

MARJORIE. Roger. He was very muscular.

CAROL. Swish! And the musician. And the stock broker. And the Jewish novelist!

MARJORIE. Oh, *they're* not like that—

CAROL. Swish! Swish! Swish! I can spot 'em a mile away. She draws 'em like flies. Too strong for real men. Too much stuff! She's got *too much stuff!* Wait, you'll see. This new one—what's his name?

MARJORIE. Alfred.

CAROL. A swish name if ever I heard one. You'll see. He'll come in. Be very polite. Very charming. Look handsome. Well dressed. Have a strong handshake. Look me right in the eye. Smile a lot. Have white teeth. Shiny hair. Look very regular. But after two or three drinks look at his wrists—he'll have trouble keeping 'em straight. Watch his lips. He'll start smacking his lips with his tongue. Watch his eyes. He'll start rolling his eyes. And his legs will go from being crossed like this— (*Wide-legged.*) to this. (*Close-legged.*) And when he gets up to start walking— (*About to mimic walk. Offstage sound of SHOTS. CAROL and MARJORIE rush to window. He struggles, but can't get it open.*) Damn! Goddamn!

MARJORIE. Hurry! (*Shots fade. Offstage siren, loud, then fading.*) They're miles away by now. You take forever.

(*Door CHIMES.*)

PATSY'S VOICE. Hey, everybody!

(*CAROL outpaces MARJORIE to door. PATSY and ALFRED enter. Confusion of ad-lib. greetings and introductions. Much excitement, laughter. CAROL more involved with his DAUGHTER than MARJORIE, who is just a touch restrained. PATSY is all-consuming. Tall, blond, vibrant, the All-American Girl.* ALFRED *is big, heavy-set and quite dour. Two cameras hang from straps around his neck.*)

PATSY. This is Alfred!

(*More ad-lib. greetings. Handshakes.*)

CAROL. Hey, you weren't in that business down there?
PATSY. What business?
CAROL. Well, from now on just be more careful.
MARJORIE. (*Eyes on* ALFRED.) I don't think we need worry any longer, dear. Patsy's finally got herself a *man!*

(*More general laughter.* CAROL *scowls.*)

PATSY. Where's my Kenny? (*Offstage sound of TOILET FLUSH.* KENNY *enters, adjusting trousers.* PATSY *swoops down on him. Ad-lib. greetings and introduction of* ALFRED. CAROL *and* KENNY *are obviously both crazy about* PATSY. *Competitive with their bids for attention.*) Alfred, this is Kenny.
MARJORIE. (*Somewhat catty.*) Alfred, have you ever seen such a madhouse? You'll have to pardon the mess.

(ALFRED *smiles diffidently.*)

CAROL. He's in the house for three minutes and she's already putting him on the spot. Have you ever seen anything like it, Alfred?

(ALFRED *smiles diffidently.*)

PATSY. Kenny! You're so handsome! I can't get over it! (*To* ALFRED.) I've always had a mad thing on my kid brother! (KENNY *clowns embarrassment.* PATSY *and* MARJORIE *laugh.* ALFRED *smiles diffidently.* CAROL *looks annoyed.*) Kenny! (*To* ALFRED.) He breaks me up!

CAROL. (*To* ALFRED.) Kenny's the comedian around here. (KENNY *sobers immediately*.) What's your pleasure, young fellow?

PATSY. Mother, what have you done to this room?

(*LIGHTS flicker and black out in apartment, and in windows across the street*.)

CAROL. If you bothered to come here more often—

MARJORIE. (*Sighs*.) Nothing special. A little bit of this. A little bit of that. (*Offstage SIRENS.* MARJORIE *lights candles. Studying* PATSY'S *face*.) I don't like your looks.

CAROL. (*Studying* PATSY.) What's the matter? The day that girl doesn't look like a million dollars—

MARJORIE. (*A studied appraisal*.) You've got black rings under your eyes.

(*LIGHTS come back up*.)

PATSY. Mother, that's eye liner.

MARJORIE. Makes you look exhausted.

KENNY. (*Studying* PATSY.) I like it.

MARJORIE. (*Blows out the candles*.) Always together!

CAROL. Do you have the slightest idea what you're talking about? She looks a million dollars!

MARJORIE. I know. It's what they're wearing today. I'm out of step. As usual.

CAROL. (*A little nervous. To* ALFRED.) What's your pleasure, young fellow?

MARJORIE. (*Critical*.) Why don't you wear your other outfit?

PATSY. What other outfit?

CAROL. Will you stop criticizing?

PATSY. What other outfit, Mother?

MARJORIE. I can't be expected to remember everything. It's not as if you still lived here.

CAROL. What's your pleasure—

KENNY. Hey, Al, want to see Patsy's old room?

PATSY. *Alfred*, Kenny. And he's not interested in **that!**

KENNY. I bet he is! Want to?

ALFRED. Maybe later.

KENNY. (*Rejected.*) Why should I care?

CAROL. (*To* KENNY.) He doesn't want to! Stop acting silly! (*To* ALFRED.) What's your pleasure, young fellow?

MARJORIE. Alfred, may I shake your hand? My mother taught us that you could tell a lot about a person by the way he shakes hands. You have a good hand. (*Flirtatious.*) Better look out, Patsy! I'll steal your boy friend! (*Releases* ALFRED's *hand. Short laugh.*) I'm only joking.

KENNY. Let me try. (*Shakes* ALFRED's *hand.*) You don't squeeze so hard. (*Disengages.*) Dad?

CAROL. This is the silliest business I've ever heard of! I think we all need drinks. What's your pleasure, young fellow?

MARJORIE. Alfred, is something the matter with your face?

ALFRED. (*To* PATSY.) Is there?

PATSY. (*Subdued annoyance.*) Just the usual assortment of bruises, Mother.

MARJORIE. What kind of talk is that? Modern talk?

PATSY. (*Not overjoyed to be on the subject.*) Alfred is always getting beat up, Mother. At least once a week. (*To* ALFRED, *annoyed.*) Or is it more?

ALFRED. (*Shakes his head to indicate it is not more.*) I don't get hurt.

MARJORIE. You don't get hurt? Carol, look at that boy! His face is a mass of bruises!

CAROL. I have asked you repeatedly never to call me Carol. (*To* PATSY.) I hate that name Carol!

MARJORIE. I have to call you something, dear.

CAROL. I don't care what you call me. Just don't call me Carol!

KENNY. Call him Harriet! (*Laughs.*) Harriet! Harriet! Oh, Harriet! Yoo-hoo! Harriet! (*Convulses himself.*)

PATSY. You're not being funny, Kenny. (*He sobers immediately.*) I love your name. I know lots of men named Carol.

KENNY. Sure. Sure. Name one.

(CAROL *glares at him.*)

PATSY. (*Thinking.*) Carol. . . .

KENNY. *Chessman!* (*Screams with laughter.*)

PATSY. King Carol of Rumania.

CAROL. That's right! King Carol! Damn it, that's right! Say, I feel like a drink. Anyone join me?

MARJORIE. I want to know why Alfred gets into these fights. I don't think that's the least bit funny.

PATSY. (*Resigned.*) Ask him!

ALFRED. (*Not interested but making an effort, mindful that this is his first attempt at conversation.*) Look. (*Long pause.* OTHERS *stir uncomfortably.*) There are lots of little people who like to start fights with big people. They hit me for a couple of minutes, they see I'm not going to fall down, they get tired and they go away.

MARJORIE. (*Agitated.*) So much tension. Rush. Rush. Rush. My mother taught us to take dainty, little steps. She'd *kill* me if she saw the stride on Patsy.

CAROL. (*Puzzled. The beginnings of contempt.*) Don't you defend yourself?

ALFRED. I ask them not to hit my cameras. They're quite good about that actually. (*Cheerful.*) Surprising!

CAROL. Let me get this straight. You just stand there and let these hooligans do whatever they want to you?

ALFRED. I'm quite strong so you needn't worry about it. At the risk of sounding arrogant this has been going on for ten years and I've yet to be knocked unconscious.

CAROL. But why don't you fight back?

ALFRED. I don't want to.

CAROL. Christ Jesus, you're not a pacifist?

PATSY. (*Warning.*) Daddy—

ALFRED. (*Slowly shakes head.*) An apathist. (*Blank stares from* CAROL *and* MARJORIE.) I want to do what I want to do, not what they want me to do.

CAROL. So you just stand there.

ALFRED. It doesn't hurt.

CAROL. Getting your face beat in doesn't hurt?

ALFRED. Not if you daydream. I daydream all through it. About my work. I imagine myself there, in the same spot, clicking off roll after roll of film, humming to myself with pleasure. I hum to myself when I work. Muggers tend to get very depressed when you hum all the while they're hitting you. There are times I get so carried away that I think I'm actually doing what I'm only dreaming I'm doing. It's not something I choose to happen. It's just one of those things you learn to live with.

PATSY. (*To* FAMILY.) Look, this is an old argument and it doesn't really concern you. Why don't we get on something else?

CAROL. (*Indignant.*) It certainly does concern me, young lady!

PATSY. (*Placating.*) Oh, Daddy—

CAROL. I want you to know it concerns me very much. (*To* ALFRED.) How do you get into these things? You must do something to get them mad—

ALFRED. No—

CAROL. Well, God damn it, you're getting *me* mad!

MARJORIE. (*Taking the heat off.*) Alfred, do you try *talking* to them?

ALFRED. (*The patient Old Pro.*) There's no way of talking someone out of beating you up if that's what he wants to do.

KENNY. (*To* PATSY.) This guy's a riot! (*She slaps at him. He playfully eludes her.*)

PATSY. Haven't we had enough of this? I'm going to make some drinks.

KENNY. Vodka and tonic.

MARJORIE. Just *one*, young man.

CAROL. I'll make them!

PATSY. No, Daddy. I want to get my hands busy. Alfred?

ALFRED. Nothing right now.

CAROL. You don't drink either. Is that right?

ALFRED. I drink beer.

CAROL. Get him a beer, Kenny.

KENNY. Why is it always my turn?

ALFRED. Not now, thanks.

CAROL. He doesn't drink.

ALFRED. I'll drink later.

CAROL. You don't drink. You don't fight.

PATSY. I fight, Daddy.

MARJORIE. Carol, leave the poor boy alone.

CAROL. (*Shouts.*) *How many times do I have to tell you—*

MARJORIE. I'm sorry. Whatever I do is wrong.

KENNY. (*Doing Bogart.*) Hey. Hey. What's dat? Dat my best goil talking? Hey. (*Hugs her from behind.*)

MARJORIE. (*Kittenish.*) Kenny! Stop it! What will Alfred think? He'll think you're always making love to your mother!

CAROL. (*Sourly.*) He *is* always making love to his mother.

MARJORIE. Well, someone has to— (*She smiles into* CAROL's *glare.*) dear.

PATSY. (*Serving drinks.*) What's this? What's this? I thought I was your best girl, Kenny?

(KENNY *tries to release* MARJORIE. *She grabs his arms and holds on.*)

MARJORIE. (*To* ALFRED.) When Patsy lived at home we used to go on like this all the time.

KENNY. (*Whining.*) Let go, Mom!

CAROL. Stop all this silliness and drink your liquor.

(MARJORIE *releases* KENNY *who goes over to* PATSY.)

MARJORIE. (*Flirtatious.*) You're an intelligent-sounding

man, Alfred. I would think if you spoke to those people quietly and sensibly they'd realize the sort of person you were and go away.

ALFRED. What can you say that's sensible to a drunk who you haven't been staring at, when he shoves you in the chest and says, "Who do you think you're staring at, Fat-Face?" If you deny you've been staring at him you've as much as called him a liar. For that you get hit. If you tell him you were staring at him because he reminds you of a kid you went to school with in Chicago, he turns out to *hate* Chicago. And for that you get hit.

MARJORIE. (*To* PATSY.) I didn't know he went to school in Chicago. Nobody tells me anything. We went to Chicago in 1946. Whereabout did you live in Chicago, Alfred?

ALFRED. The South Side.

MARJORIE. I'm not comfortable eating away from home. Well, that's another story. Does your family still live there?

ALFRED. I don't know.

CAROL. You don't know! What kind of answer is that? You don't know! That's the silliest answer I've ever heard!

ALFRED. I haven't kept up contact.

(CAROL *frowns, disapproving.*)

MARJORIE. There seems to be so little cohesiveness in families today. *We* never went anywhere. We were too unsophisticated to know that home wouldn't serve. (*To* PATSY.) Today they run off here, they run off there—

KENNY. (*Hugs her.*) I'll never leave you, Mom.

CAROL. Will you two break it up? How about another round? Name your poison, Alfred.

MARJORIE. (*Sadly*.) We've had our share of tragedy—
PATSY. (*Warning*.) Mother—

(*PHONE rings. CAROL starts for it. MARJORIE beats him to it.*)

MARJORIE. Let me, dear. It's never for you. Hello. (*Amplified sound of heavy BREATHING*.) Hello. Hello. Who is this? Hello. (PATSY *starts toward her*.) The most curious business. Hello.

(PATSY *takes the phone. Listens. Hangs up.*)

PATSY. (*To* MARJORIE.) You get it too.
CAROL. What? (PATSY *looks toward* MARJORIE *who smiles, but does not answer*.) What?
MARJORIE. Never mind, dear. It's not important.

(CAROL *frustrated*. PATSY *goes to him*.)

PATSY. The Breather, Daddy. Do you get many of these, Mother?
MARJORIE. He's the pleasantest of the lot. You should hear the ones who *talk!* I grit my teeth, turn my ears *right* off, and wait politely for them, 'til they've finished their business.
CAROL. (*Exasperated*.) Will somebody please explain to me—?
PATSY. I get them every night. I suppose everyone does. You know, Daddy—these odd-balls who call you up at all hours and just *breathe* at you.
CAROL. (*Appalled*.) Late at night? They breathe at you? (*To* ALFRED.) And you don't fight back?!

(*Door CHIME*.)

MARJORIE. I'll get it! (*Crosses to door. Opens peephole*.) Who is it? I'm sorry, I can't understand you! Will

you please stand closer to the peephole? I can't see you—
Please take your hand off the peephole. I warn you, I'm
calling the doorman! (PATSY *starts for the door.* MAR-
JORIE *shuts the peephole, intercepts her. Returns, mus-
ing.*) If it happens once, it happens a dozen times a day.
And we gave that doorman fifteen dollars for Christmas.

(PATSY *protectively puts arms around her.* MARJORIE
lightly shrugs if off.)

CAROL. (*To* ALFRED.) *What are you going to do if
you're on the street with my daughter?*

PATSY. Don't be silly, Daddy. I'm quite capable of taking care of myself.

KENNY. (*Proudly.*) She's as strong as an ox. When we
were kids we used to wrestle all the time. I always lost.

PATSY. (*Enjoying herself.*) Daddy, I assure you, no
one's going to pick on me. I'm a big, strapping girl! I
don't daydream, and I *do* hit back. When I take Alfred
home every night I guarantee you there's no trouble.

CAROL. You let *her* take you home?

PATSY. He doesn't *let* me. He doesn't have anything to
say about it. Every time I leave him alone somebody in
this crazy city mugs him. Once I have him safely married— (CAROL *and* KENNY *wince.*) I won't let him out
of my sight for five minutes. (*Pinches* ALFRED.) He's too
cute to get beat up—by anyone but me.

(*Throws playful, but entirely masculine punch at* ALFRED.
He smiles happily as it connects. KENNY *exits.*)

MARJORIE. Aren't they adorable?

CAROL. (*Quietly to* MARJORIE.) What did I tell you
about him, huh? Didn't I predict?

MARJORIE. I think he's very sweet.

CAROL. That's a sure sign. You think they're *all* sweet.
I'll be damned— (*Louder.*) if I'd let myself stand by and
let a woman fight my battles for me.

PATSY. (*Hugging* CAROL *from behind.*) They don't make frontier fighters like my father any more.

MARJORIE. (*Looks about.*) Kenny! (*Shakes head in exasperation. Smiles seductively at* ALFRED.) Alfred, would you mind giving me a hand?

(*They exit.*)

CAROL. (*Delighted.*) Come on. Stop being silly. Cut it out.

PATSY. (*Playful, squeezing tighter.*) Let's see how good you are, tiger. Break my grip! Come on!

(*Momentary look of panic in* CAROL'S *eyes.* PATSY *releases him. They laugh.*)

CAROL. (*Slaps her cheek playfully.*) Who's my baby girl, eh? (*Suddenly serious.*) I wish you had as much brains as you have brawn.

PATSY. You don't like him, do you, Daddy?

CAROL. Don't put words in my mouth.

PATSY. Then you *do* like him?

CAROL. I want to know more about him before I make up my mind—

PATSY. Not to like him.

CAROL. Don't bully me, young lady. You know I don't like it when you bully me.

PATSY. You *love* it when I bully you.

CAROL. (*Chuckles.*) You're too damned fast for the old man. (*Slaps her cheek playfully.*) But I know a thing or two. (*Deadly serious.*) Never settle for less.

PATSY. Daddy, I'm *not!*

CAROL. Never sell yourself short.

PATSY. Oh, Daddy, when have I *ever*—

CAROL. The right man will come along.

PATSY. Daddy, I'm twenty-seven. The right men all got married two years ago. They won't get their first divorce for another five years and I just don't have the time, the inclination, or the kind of looks that can afford to wait.

CAROL. I don't want to hear you knocking yourself. You've got ten people working under you! (*Proudly.*) You're five foot eight!

PATSY. After a while it doesn't *matter* that you can do everything better than everyone else. I've been the best for years now, and all it comes down to is that I'm efficient.

CAROL. You don't know what you're talking about. You're very popular.

PATSY. When they want a woman they can collapse without shame in front of—they come to me.

CAROL. Why not? You're trusted!

PATSY. Oh, to meet a man who *is* ashamed to collapse in front of me! Daddy, I get dizzy spells from being so strong; I get migraine from being so damnably dependable. I'm tired of being Mother Earth! Alfred's the *only* man I know who isn't waiting for me to save him. Don't you know how that makes me feel? (CAROL *shakes his head.*) God help me, I've got to save him!

(*Embraces* CAROL *who blissfully returns embrace.* ALFRED *enters uncorking wine, surveys scene.* CAROL *disengages.*)

MARJORIE. (*Enters wheeling serving cart.*) *Come An' Git It!* Alfred, my mother always used to say that to us children at mealtimes. I've always found it a charming family tradition. So I say, "Come An' Git It" to our children. I dream of the day when I can hear Patsy say "Come An' Git It" to her children. (*To Offstage.*) *Kenny!* Didn't you hear me say "Come An' Git It"? Or do you need a special invitation?

KENNY. (*Offstage.*) In a minute!

MARJORIE. Not a minute, young man! Right now!— (*To* ALFRED.) It's so stuffy in here. Alfred, would you open the window like a good fellow? (*Sound of TOILET FLUSH.* CAROL *rises.*) No, I asked Alfred, dear.

(KENNY *enters with paperback, passes* CAROL, *who outpaces* ALFRED *to window.*)

CAROL. (*Struggling with window.*) It's all right. It's perfectly all right. (*Gives up.*) Son of a bitch! (*To AL-FRED.*) The son of a bitch refuses to open!

(ALFRED *gives strong jerk. Window opens. TRAFFIC, CONSTRUCTION and AIRPLANE noise.*)

MARJORIE. Thank you, Alfred. (*To* CAROL.) You see, I had my reasons.

(*Light film of SOOT wafts through window.*)

CAROL. I loosened it!
KENNY. He loosened it! That's a riot! (*Convulses himself.*)
CAROL. (*Slams window shut. To* KENNY.) Now *you* open it! (KENNY *airily dismisses him.*) No, you're the smart one around here! Let's see you open it.
MARJORIE. I spent the whole day cooking. Can't we eat now and open and close windows later?
CAROL. It won't take a second. Well, young man, are you going to try or are you just going to sit back and laugh at the earnest efforts of your betters? (KENNY, *with arrogant mockery, rises, and in a fey manner, tries and fails, to open window. Shrugs, smiles and ambles back to table.* ALFRED *and* CAROL *follow.* ALL *sit.*) You're not so smart now, are you?
MARJORIE. Will someone please open the window? (PATSY *leaps up before* ALFRED *can rise, strides to window, kicks off heels, jerks window open. NOISE and DUST.* KENNY *and* CAROL *bend over their soup, embarrassed.* PATSY *returns to table.*) When Patsy lived at home I always knew I had someone to do my heavy lifting for me. I was always too petite. (PATSY *shrinks over her soup plate. All quietly eat.*) You don't know what a pleasure it is to have my family all together this way. (*LIGHTS flicker, black out, as before. Sound of EATING.*) Do you know that in last year's *big* power failure

some people stood in the subways, in total darkness, for as long as four hours without bringing their newspapers down from in front of their faces? (*Long silence. EATING sounds.* MARJORIE *lights candles.*) It would be nice if someone else, on occasion, would think of lighting the candles. Kenny, come back here. (KENNY, *about to exit, returns carrying paperback.*) I'm the watchdog around here, Alfred. I can imagine what Patsy must have told you about me.

PATSY. (*Bored.*) Must you, Mother?

(*They exchange long stares.* MARJORIE *rises and exits.*)

CAROL. (*Up quickly.*) I'm going to make myself another drink.

KENNY. Make me one.

PATSY. Me too.

ALFRED. Scotch neat.

(CAROL *stops, stare at him. Goes over to bar, grinning. Offstage sound of TOILET FLUSH.*)

MARJORIE. (*Enters carrying photographs.*) It's gotten a little chilly in here— (KENNY *up before anyone can move. Slams down window.* CAROL *serves drinks.* MARJORIE *frowns as* PATSY *accepts drink.*) That's your second tonight, isn't it? And I suppose you're still smoking as much? (PATSY *salutes with glass. Drains it.*) Drinks like a fish. Smokes like a chimney. (PATSY *mocks cough spasm.*) It's the ones who think they're indestructible who do the most damage to themselves. Kenny, is that a new drink? (KENNY *bolts drink.* MARJORIE *shakes head, looks wearily at* CAROL. *He bolts drink, scratches his hand nervously. To* ALFRED, *with photographs.*) You're a photographer, Alfred, so I thought you'd be interested in seeing these pictures of Patsy's dead brother, Steve.

(PATSY *covers her face with her hands.*)

ALFRED. He looks very handsome in his swimsuit.

MARJORIE. He won five gold cups. He was four years older than Patsy.

KENNY. Seven years older than me!

ALFRED. He looks very handsome in his baseball uniform.

MARJORIE. He only pitched no-hitters.

ALFRED. (*Handing back pictures.*) Thank you for letting me see them.

MARJORIE. This one was taken after he came home from the war, a hero.

ALFRED. He looks very handsome in his uniform. What do these double bars signify?

MARJORIE. He was a captain. A hero. He bombed Tokyo. When his country called on him to serve again he bombed Korea. A brilliant future in electronics, not an enemy in the world, whoever dreamed he'd be shot down in his tracks on the corner of 97th and Amsterdam Avenue. (*Gathers pictures.*) But I won't bore you with our tragedy.

PATSY. (*Explodes.*) Damn it, Mother! Must I go through this every time I bring a man home to dinner? (MARJORIE *sobs, rushes off.*) Patsy's done it again!

KENNY. (*Admiringly.*) Boy, I'd be killed if I ever talked like that.

CAROL. I don't approve of your behavior, young lady. She worked long and hard and imaginatively over this dinner. (PATSY *puts cigarette in her mouth.*) And she's right about your smoking too much, God damn it!

(PATSY *turns to* CAROL, *cigarette in mouth, waiting for light. He resists for a moment, then lights it.*)

PATSY. (*In command.*) Thank you. (CAROL *scratches his hand. Softly to* ALFRED.) I'm sorry you had to be subjected to this, honey. (*To* CAROL, *taking his hand, placating.*) Alfred knows all about Steve, Daddy.

(CAROL *revives.*)

ALFRED. They still don't have any idea who did it?

CAROL. That's *all* right. The boys down at Homicide have worked long and hard and imaginatively on this case. (*With pride.*) Many have become close, personal friends.

(*TOILET flushes. MARJORIE enters, eyes red, but smiling. She is clutching a handkerchief. KENNY rises and exits in her direction.*)

MARJORIE. We can't disappoint our guest with only one helping.

ALFRED. No, thank you, Mrs. Newquist. I've had plenty.

PATSY. (*Ingratiating.*) It was delicious, Mother!

CAROL. It was delicious!

MARJORIE. Kenny! Where are you?

KENNY. (*Offstage, muffled.*) *It was delicious!*

MARJORIE. (*To ALFRED.*) A big man like you. Now, don't just stand on politeness—

ALFRED. No. I'm really quite full, thank you.

MARJORIE. (*To PATSY.*) Well, then I'll have to turn to my best customer.

PATSY. I couldn't eat another bite. It was delicious.

CAROL. I couldn't eat another bite. It was delicious.

KENNY. (*Offstage, muffled.*) *I couldn't eat another bite. It was delicious!* (*Toilet FLUSH. He enters, with paperback.*) I could use another drink, though. (*Detours on his way back from bar to surreptitiously pick up* PATSY'S *shoes in front of window. Takes them to his seat.*)

CAROL. (*Rises.*) I think I'll have another. (*At bar.*) Patsy?

PATSY. (*Rises.*) Leave out the water this time. (*Goes to bar.*)

ALFRED. Scotch neat.

MARJORIE. Well, it's a special occasion.

PATSY. (*Looks around.*) Where the devil did I leave my shoes?

(KENNY *looks away.*)

MARJORIE. (*Gathering photographs from table.*) I'd better put these in a safe place before someone spills liquor on them. I'm sorry to have taken your time, Alfred. Knowing you were a photographer I thought you'd be interested. (*Waits for response. There is none.*) Exactly what sort of work do you do? Portraits?

ALFRED. No.

PATSY. (*Returns protectively. Hands* ALFRED *drink.*) Stop cross-examining him, Mother.

MARJORIE. I don't know why everything I do is wrong. Alfred, do you object to my asking you about your work?

ALFRED. It's not all that interesting, actually.

MARJORIE. You don't do portraits?

ALFRED. No.

MARJORIE. Do you do magazine photography?

ALFRED. No.

PATSY. Has somebody got a cigarette?

MARJORIE. (*To* PATSY.) Must you? Can't you give in to me just this once? (CAROL *sits, hands* PATSY *cigarette.* KENNY *lights it. Barely in control, to* ALFRED.) Advertising photography?

ALFRED. Well, I used to. I don't any more.

CAROL. Fashion photography? (*Nudges* KENNY.)

KENNY. (*Rolls eyes.*) Woo! Woo!

(CAROL *and* KENNY *exchange joyful glances. Stifle laughs.*)

ALFRED. It's sort of complicated. Are you sure you want to hear?

PATSY. You may as well—

ALFRED. Well, I began as a commercial photographer—

PATSY. He began as a painter.

ALFRED. A very bad painter.

PATSY. Says you!

CAROL. *For Christ sakes, will you let the boy finish!*

(ALL, *including* CAROL, *surprised by the outburst.*)

ALFRED. I began as a commercial photographer—
CAROL. What kind of commercial photographer?
ALFRED. —and was doing sort of well at it.
PATSY. *Sort* of well! You should see his portfolio. He's
had work in *Holiday, Esquire, The New Yorker, Vogue*—
CAROL. *Vogue!*
KENNY. (*Rolls eyes.*) Woo! Woo!

(*He and* CAROL *exchange nudges, joyful glances.* PATSY
glares. They subside.)

ALFRED. It's an overrated business. But after a couple
of years at it, things began to go wrong. I began losing
my people. Somehow I got my heads chopped off. Or out
of focus. Or terrible expressions on my models. I'd have
them examining a client's product like this. (*Expression
of distaste.*) The agencies began to wonder if I didn't have
some editorial motive in mind. Well, of course, it wasn't
true. But once they'd *planted* the idea—I couldn't help
thinking of plane crashes every time I shot an airline ad,
deaths on the highway every time I shot an automobile
ad, and power failures—when I shot Con Edison ads.
(*LIGHTS go out.*)
MARJORIE. I don't mean to interrupt, dear. (*Lights
match and candles.*) "How far better it is to light a candle
than curse the darkness." My mother told us that. Go on.
ALFRED. Well, my career suffered. But there was nothing
I could do about it. The harder I tried to straighten out the
fuzzier my people got and the clearer my objects. Soon my
people disappeared entirely. I can't tell you what hap-
pened; they just somehow never came out. But the objects
I was shooting— (*Snaps fingers.*) brilliantly clear.
(*LIGHTS come back on.*) So I began to do a lot of cata-
logue work. (MARJORIE *blows out candles.*) Pictures of

medical instruments, things like that. Boring, but it kept me alive. There was—well—the best way to describe it is —a *seductiveness* I was able to draw out of inanimate things that other photographers didn't seem able to get. I suppose the real break came with the I.B.M. show. They had me shoot thirty of their new models. They hired a gallery and had a computer show. One hundred and twenty color pictures of computers. It got some very strange— (*Whimsical smile.*) notices, the upshot of which was that the advertising business went thing crazy, and I became commercial again.

MARJORIE. You must be extremely talented.

(CAROL *mimes man blowing his own horn.*)

ALFRED. (*More to himself than to family.*) I got *sick* of it! Where the hell are standards? That's what I kept asking myself. Those people will take anything! If I gave them a picture of shit they'd give me an award for it!

(ALL *stiffen,* PATSY *looks wary.*)

MARJORIE. Language, young man!
ALFRED. Mm? So that's what I do now.
CAROL. (*Hesitantly.*) What?
ALFRED. Take pictures of shit.
MARJORIE. Language! Language! This is *my* table!
ALFRED. I don't mean to offend you, Mrs. Newquist. I've been shooting shit for a year now, and I've already won a half dozen awards.
MARJORIE. (*Slowly thaws.*) Awards?
ALFRED. And Harper's Bazaar want me to do its Spring issue.
KENNY. (*Rolling eyes.*) Woo! Woo!
CAROL. (*Angry to* KENNY.) *Don't kid!*
MARJORIE. That's a very respectable publication. (*Rises shakily, gathers up dishes.*) It all sounds very impressive.

(*Exits shakily with serving cart.* CAROL *up quickly, about
to speak when PHONE rings. He goes for it, all the
while glaring to* ALFRED.)

CAROL. Hello. (*Amplified BREATHING.*) Look, I don't
know who you are but you're not dealing with helpless
women now! *You people! You young people today! Destroy! Destroy! When are you going to find time to build?
In MY day we couldn't afford telephones to breathe in!
You ought to get down on your hands and knees and be
grateful!* Why isn't anybody *grateful?!* (PATSY *takes re-
ceiver away. Hangs up.*) Excuse me. (*Exits.*)

PATSY. Kenny, would you mind—

KENNY. (*Grins.*) It's my house.

PATSY. (*Threatening.*) Kenny! (PATSY *starts for him.
He jumps up from table, grabbing his drink and runs out.
He has on* PATSY's *heels. Offstage sound of distant
SIREN.*) Well, my friend—

ALFRED. They asked me what I did for a living.
(*Shrugs.*)

PATSY. (*Gives him a long stare.*) I don't know what to
do with you. You're the toughest reclamation job *I've* ever
had.

ALFRED. You might try retiring on your laurels. You've
reformed five fags in a row, why press your luck with a
nihilist?

PATSY. *Because you're wrong!* Alfred, every age has
problems. And people somehow manage TO BE HAPPY!
I'm sorry, I don't mean to bully you. (*Pause.*) Yes, I do
mean to bully you. Alfred, do you know how I wake up
every morning of my life? With a smile on my face. And
for the rest of the day I come up against an unending
series of challenges to wipe that smile off my face. The
breather calls . . . ex-boyfriends call to tell me they're
getting married. . . . Someone tries to break into the
apartment while I'm dressing. . . . There's a drunk asleep
in the elevator. . . . Three minutes after I'm out on the

street my camel coat turns brown. . . . The subway
stalls. . . . The man standing next to me presses his body
against mine. . . . The up elevator jams. . . . Rumors
start buzzing around the office that we're about to be
automated. . . . The down elevator jams. . . . All the
taxis are off-duty. . . . The air on Lexington Avenue
is purple. . . . A man tries to pick me up on the bus. . . .
Another man follows me home. . . . I step in the door
and the breather's on the phone. . . . Isn't that enough
to wipe the smile off anybody's face? Well, it doesn't
wipe it off *mine!* Because for every bad thing there are
two good things. No, FOUR good things! There are
friends . . . and a wonderful job . . . and tennis . . .
and skiing . . . and traveling . . . and musicals . . .
and driving in the country . . . and flying your own airplane . . . and staying up all night to see the sun rise.
. . . (ALFRED *goes into his daydream.*) Alfred, come back
here! (*Long pause.*) Alfred, if everything is to hopeless—
why do anything?

ALFRED. Okay.

PATSY. That's why you don't hit back?

ALFRED. There isn't much point, is there?

PATSY. (*Explodes.*) *Do you know what you're talking
about? Do you have the slightest idea—* (*Catches herself.*) I always talk like my father when I'm in this house.
Alfred— (*Long pause.*) if you feel that way about
things— (*Long pause.*) why get married?

ALFRED. You said you wanted to.

PATSY. (*Turns away.*) I find this a very unpleasant
conversation.

ALFRED. (*Dryly.*) Patsy, let's not turn this into a
"critical conversation," just because you're not getting
your way. *I'm* for getting married.

PATSY. Thanks.

ALFRED. (*After a long pause.*) So it is a "critical conversation." (*He starts off.*)

PATSY. Alfred! (*Starts after him, muttering to herself.*)

He doesn't know how to fight; that's why I'm not winning. (*Exits. Brings him back.*) Damn it! Aren't you willing to battle over anything? Even me?

ALFRED *and* PATSY. There isn't much point, is there? (*She bear-hugs him.*)

PATSY. At least say you love me. I know:

ALFRED *and* PATSY. I'm not sure I know what love is.

PATSY. (*Slaps him in the stomach.*) Okay. The gauntlet's flung! You've had it, buster! I'm going to marry you, make you give me a house, entrap you into a half dozen children, and seduce you into a life so remorselessly satisfying that within two years under my management you'll come to me with a camera full of baby pictures and say: "Life Can Be Beautiful!"

ALFRED. And ugly. More often ugly.

PATSY. You'll give me a piano to sing around. And a fireplace to lie in front of. And each and every Christmas we will send out *personalized* Christmas cards—with a group family portrait on the front—taken by *Alfred Chamberlain.* Daddy! Mother! I have an announcement! (CAROL *and* MARJORIE *rush in. Sound of toilet FLUSH.* KENNY *rushes in.*) Alfred and I are getting married! (CAROL *and* KENNY *freeze.*) Next week!

(CAROL *sits down heavily.*)

MARJORIE. (*Beaming.*) I've always dreamed of a wedding in my living room! Oh, there's so much to do. (*Kisses them.*) You've got yourself a fine young man. And so accomplished! We'll have to let Dr. Paterson know right away—

ALFRED. (*To* PATSY.) Who?

PATSY. The minister, dopey.

ALFRED. (*To* MARJORIE, *who is picking up phone.*) Mrs. Newquist— (*Sound of amplified BREATHING.* MARJORIE *quickly hangs up. Picks up again and begins to dial.*) Mrs. Newquist, when you speak to the Minister you'd better tell him—we don't want any mention of God in the ceremony.

CAROL. I'm going to have you arrested.

(ALL *freeze, stare at* ALFRED.)

ACT ONE

SCENE 2

The NEWQUIST *apartment, one month later.* ALFRED, PATSY, CAROL *and* MARJORIE *sit quietly.* CAROL *looks at his watch, rises, begins to pace.* PATSY *places a calming hand on* ALFRED'S *arm.* MARJORIE, *the only one unperturbed, smiles gamely. Door CHIME.* CAROL *crosses to door.*

MARJORIE. Ask who it is first!

(CAROL *fights with locks, opens door. The* JUDGE *enters, a portly, well-dressed man of about Carol's age.*)

CAROL. (*Softly as if at a wake.*) Jerry. You don't know how I appreciate this.

(JUDGE *nods, accepts* CAROL'S *handshake, looks at his watch.*)

JUDGE. Nice to see you again, Mrs. Newquist. Are these the youngsters? (CAROL *nods.*) No God in the ceremony. Does she live away from home? (CAROL *nods.*) It begins there.

MARJORIE. You'll have to pardon the mess, Judge Stern.

JUDGE. You have a second girl, don't you, Carol?

CAROL. A boy.

JUDGE. A son!

CAROL. A boy.

MARJORIE. (*To* PATSY *and* ALFRED.) Children, this is—

CAROL. I'll do it—Judge Jerome M. Stern, one of my oldest and dearest—

JUDGE. I don't have much time. If the grownups will please excuse us . . .

(*Looks to* CAROL *and* MARJORIE, *who reluctantly start to exit as* KENNY *enters.*)

MARJORIE. Out, young man.

KENNY. Why can't I ever—

(MARJORIE *shoves him. They exit together.*)

JUDGE. (*Stares at* ALFRED *and* PATSY *for a long moment.*) Sit down please. (*They remain standing.*) I can't talk unless I'm the tallest. (PATSY *sits, and eases* ALFRED *down beside her.*) No God in the ceremony, m'm? You've been turned down quite a lot, haven't you? Surprising, isn't it, how the name of God is still respected in this town? (*Studies* PATSY.) Carol Newquist's daughter. (*Sighs.*) Your father and me go back a long ways, young lady. He's done me a lot of favors. Got me tickets to shows— (*Sighs. Shakes head.*) I'd *like* to help him out— (*Shakes head.*) My mother, thank God she's not alive today, landed in this country sixty-five years ago. Four infants in her arms. Kissed the sidewalk the minute she got off the boat, she was so happy to be here. To be out of Russia alive. Across the ocean alive. More dead than alive if you want to know the truth. Sixteen days in the steerage. Fifteen people got consumption. Five died. My father, thank God he's not alive today, came over two years earlier, sixty-seven years ago. Worked like a son of a bitch to earn our passage— (*To* PATSY.) Pardon my French. You don't want God in the ceremony, so you're probably familiar with it. My father worked four-

teen hours a day in a sweat shop on lower Broadway.
Number 315. Our first apartment was a five-flight walkup,
four and a half room cold-water flat. With the bathtub in
the kitchen and the toilet down the hall. 142 Hester
Street. Three families used the toilet. An Italian family.
A colored family. A Jewish family. Three families with
different faiths, but one thing each of those families had
in common. They had in common the sacrifices each of
them had to make to get where they were. What they
had in common was *persecution!* So they weren't so glib
about God. God was in my mother's every conversation
about how she got her family out of Russia, thank God,
in one piece. About the pogroms. The steerage. About
those who *didn't* make it. Got sick and died. Who could
they ask for help? If not God, then who? *The Great Society? The Department of Welfare? Travelers' Aid?* Mind
you, I'm a good Democrat, I'm not knocking these things.
Although sometimes—there weren't any handouts in those
days. This city was a—a—a concrete jungle to the families
that came here. They had to carve homes and lives out of
concrete—cold concrete! You think they didn't call on
God, these poor suffering greenhorns? You see the suit I'm
wearing? Expensive? Custom-made? My father, thank
God he's not alive today, worked sixteen hours a day in
a shop on Broome Street and his artistry for a tenth of
what you pay today makes meat loaf out this suit. 145
dash 147 Broome Street. So tired, so broken in spirit
when he headed home at night, climbed six flights of stairs
to the three room unheated cold-water flat the five of us
were crowded in—171 Attorney Street—that he did not
have the strength to eat. *The man did not have the
strength to eat.* What was God to my father? I'll tell you
—sit down, I'm not finished! I'll tell you what God was
to my father! God got my father up those six and a half
flights of stairs, not counting the stoop, every night. God
got my mother, worn gray from lying to her children

about a better tomorrow she didn't believe in, up each morning with enough of the failing strength that finally deserted her last year in Miami Beach at the age of ninety-one, to face another day of hopelessness and despair. 3135 Biscayne Boulevard. God. Do you know how old I was when I first had to go out to work? Look at these hands? The hands of a judge? The hands of a professional man? Not on your sweet life! The hands of a *worker!* I *worked!* These hands toiled from the time I was nine, strike that, seven. Every morning up at five, dressing in the pitch black, to run down seven flights of stairs, thirteen steps to a flight—I'll never forget them—to run five blocks to the Washington market, unpacking crates for seventy-five cents a week. A dollar if I worked Sundays. Maybe! Based on the goodness of the boss's heart. Where was my God then? Where on those bitter-cold mornings, with my hands so blue with frostbite they looked like lady's gloves, was God? Here! In my heart! Where He was, has been, will always be! Till the day they carry me feet first out of these chambers—knock wood God grant it's soon. My first murder trial—where are you going? I'm not finished!

ALFRED. (*At door.*) You're not going to marry us.

JUDGE. I'm not finished! Don't be a smart punk! (ALFRED *exits.*) You're a know-it-all wise guy smart punk, aren't you? I've seen your kind! *You'll come up before me again!* (PATSY *exits.* CAROL *and* MARJORIE *enter.* JUDGE *looks at his watch. Very coldly, after long pause.*) He made me very late.

BLACKOUT

ACT ONE

SCENE 3

The Newquist apartment decorated for a wedding.
GUESTS *having their pictures taken. Three GUN-
SHOTS heard from window.*

GUEST ONE. Where is it?

GUEST TWO. Up there.

GUEST THREE. Where?

GUEST FOUR. There.

GUEST FIVE. He's got a rifle.

GUEST SIX. Somebody call the police.

GUEST TWO. He's only a kid.

GUEST THREE. Kids can kill.

GUEST SIX. I think somebody should call the police.

GUEST SEVEN. I think Carol should call the police.

GUEST FOUR. An old lady got murdered in my building in front of thirty witnesses.

GUEST THREE. And everyone just stood there, right?

GUEST ONE. Call the police. (GUESTS *begin to drift away from window. Two more SHOTS, which they ignore.*)

GUEST THREE. I learned to kill with the edge of a rolled up newspaper.

GUEST SEVEN. I carry a hunting knife. (*The Family enters.* GUESTS *applaud.*)

CAROL. (*An apologetic smile.*) Nothing like a little excitement, is there? (*Family proceeds to mix and talk with* GUESTS.)

MARJORIE. Aren't they an attractive couple? He's so big. It's wonderful to marry a big man. There are so many complications when you marry a man shorter than yourself.

CAROL. I gave them twenty-five hundred. It's just a token.

MARJORIE. And she's so big herself. Many's the time I gave up hope she'd find a man bigger than she is.

CAROL. Twenty-five hundred—

MARJORIE. Or heavier. It's always amazed me the size of her. I've always been such a little peanut.

ALFRED. No. My family's not here.

MARJORIE. You'd think almost anybody I'd married would have to be bigger than me; well, that's the way life works out.

KENNY. I haven't made up my mind. I may go into teaching.

MARJORIE. He's a world-famous photographer, you know. He does collages for *Harper's Bazaar*. (*General LAUGHTER.* MARJORIE *looks around to see what she is missing.*) And he's terribly independent. I always thought Patsy was independent but this time I think she's met her match.

PATSY. Well, the first year at least we'll live at my place.

MARJORIE. No God in the ceremony, he says. Yes God in the ceremony, she says. Well, you see who won that one.

CAROL. Twenty-five hundred—

ALFRED. No. My family isn't here.

MARJORIE. I would never have the nerve to stand up to her. Her father has never stood up to her. Her brother has never stood up to her. But this time she didn't get her way. (*Gaily.*) There's not going to be any God in the ceremony.

KENNY. What I really want to do is direct films.

MARJORIE. Poor children, these past few weeks they've really had a rough time of it. Nobody wanted to marry them. Even the state of New York has God in the cere-mony. They looked everywhere.

ALFRED. No. My family's not here.

MARJORIE. Ethical Culture told them they didn't have to have God in the ceremony but they did have to have ethical culture in the ceremony.

PATSY. I plan to go on working into my eighth month.

MARJORIE. Finally, they found this man— (DUPAS *enters.*) Alfred found him really—there he is now— Reverend Dupas. (*Pronounced Doo-pah.*)

ALFRED. (*Escorting* PATSY *over to* DUPAS.) Henry.

(Mimed greetings and handshakes.)

MARJORIE. He doesn't have much of a handshake but Alfred says he's very well established in Greenwich Village. He's pastor of the First Existential Church—the one that has that sign in front—that says—

DUPAS. (*To* ALFRED.) My bike wouldn't start up.

MARJORIE. "Christ died for our sins. Dare we make his martyrdom meaningless by not committing them?"

CAROL. (*To* DUPAS. *With feigned good cheer.*) No atheists in foxholes these days, eh, Reverend? They've all gone into the ministry.

MARJORIE. Two Sundays ago he gave a sermon on the moral affirmation in Alfred's photographs.

CAROL. Can I see you for a minute in private, Reverend? (*Leads him off.*)

KENNY. (*Starts off.*) Hey, that's *my* room.

MARJORIE. They'll be right out, dear.

KENNY. How do they know I don't have to go in there? (*Starts off.* MARJORIE *blocks his way.*) I need a handkerchief! I've got a right to go into my own room!

MARJORIE. (*Conciliatory.*) Why don't you go into the bathroom, dear?

KENNY. (*To* PATSY.) Why can't you do your things in your own room?

PATSY. Kenny— (*Reaches for him. He turns away.*) Why are you mad at me?

(KENNY *storms away. Phone rings.* KENNY *gets it. Amplified BREATHING.*)

KENNY. (*Into phone.*) Faggot! (*Hangs up.*)

DUPAS. (*To* ALFRED.) Your father-in-law wants me to sneak the Deity into the ceremony.

ALFRED. What did you tell him?

DUPAS. He offered me a lot of money. I told him I'd make my decision in a few minutes. (DUPAS *checks* CAROL'S *whereabouts. He is across room being congrat-*

ulated, *scratching his hand and staring intently at*
Dupas.) If it's all right with you I'd like to take the
money and then *not* mention the Deity. First Existential
can use the money.

ALFRED. He'll stop the check.

Dupas. I thought he might. Still, it would serve as a
lesson.

ALFRED. I don't know what to tell you, Henry—

Dupas. Well, we'll see—

(Crosses over to CAROL. *They exit.)*

KENNY. (*Starts off.*) I need something out of my room.

MARJORIE. Kenny! (*She blocks his way.* KENNY *tries
to charge past her. She intercepts, and they begin to
struggle. With forced gaiety.*) Ha! Ha! Look, everybody!
We're dancing.

(CAROL *and* DUPAS *enter. Wrestling match breaks up.*
CAROL, *hiding triumph, crosses over to* ALFRED.)

CAROL. (*Slaps him on the back.*) Nervous, young fellow? (ALFRED *turns to look for* PATSY. CAROL *takes him
by the arm.*) I've been looking forward to this day for a
long, long time. It would only take one thing more to
make it perfect. (ALFRED *smiles politely. Looks for*
PATSY. CAROL *squeezes his arm.*) To hear you call me
Dad.

ALFRED. I didn't call my own father Dad.

CAROL. What did you call him?

ALFRED. I didn't call him anything. The occasion never
came up. (*Amiably.*) I could call you Carol.

CAROL. (*Winces.*) Look, if it's this God business that's
bothering you I'm willing to be open-minded. I wouldn't
let this on to Marjorie and the kids: (*Winks.*) I don't believe in God. But to me it's not a matter of belief in
God. It's a matter of belief in institutions. I have a great
belief in institutions. You couldn't concede me *one* Dad?

(*No response.*) Not all the time—but every once in a while— "Hello, Dad"— "How are you, Dad?"—

DUPAS. May we proceed?

CAROL. "You like some of my tobacco, Dad?"— (ALFRED *tries to free his arm.* CAROL *hangs on, hisses.*) I want an answer!

(PATSY *crosses, kisses* CAROL, *takes* ALFRED *away.* ALL *take their positions for the ceremony.*)

DUPAS. You all know why we're here. There is often so much sham about this business of marriage. Everyone accepts it. Ritual. That's why I was so heartened when Alfred asked me to perform this ceremony. He has certain beliefs that I assume you all know. He is an atheist, which is perfectly all right. Really it is. I happen not to be, but inasmuch as this ceremony connotates an abandonment of ritual in the search for truth, I agreed to perform it. First, let me state frankly to you, Alfred, and to you, Patricia, that of the two hundred marriages I have performed, all but seven have failed. So the odds are not good. We don't like to admit it, especially at the wedding ceremony, but it's in the back of all our minds, isn't it? How long will it last? We all think that, don't we? We don't like to bring it out in the open but we all think that. Don't we? Well, I say why not bring it out in the open? *Why* does one decide to marry? Social pressure? Boredom? Loneliness? Sexual appeasement? Um, love? I do not put any of these reasons down. Each in its own way is adequate. Each is all right. I married a musician last year who wanted to get married in order to stop masturbating. (GUESTS *stir.*) Please don't be startled. I am not putting it down. That marriage did not work. But the man is separated, and still masturbating—but he is at peace with himself. He tried society's way. So you see, it was not a mistake, it turned out all right. Last month I married a novelist to a painter with everyone at the wedding under the influence of hallucinogenic drugs. The drug quickened our mental responses but slowed our physical responses. It took two days to perform the ceremony. But never had the words had so much meaning. *That* marriage should last. Still, if it does not—well, that will be all right. For don't you see, *any* step one takes is useful. Is positive, *has* to be positive, because it is part of life. And negation of the previously taken step is positive. It too is part of life. And in this light, and *only* in this light, should marriage be regarded. As a small, single step. If it works . . . fine! If it fails . . . fine! Look elsewhere for satisfaction. Perhaps to more marriages, as many as one likes . . . fine! To homosexuality . . . fine! To drug addiction . . . I won't put it down. Each of these is an *answer* . . . for *somebody*. For Alfred, today's answer is Patsy. For Patsy, today's answer is Alfred. I won't put them down for that. What, I implore you both, Alfred and Patricia, to dwell on as I ask the questions required by the State of New York in order to legally bind you— sinister phrase, that—is that not only are the *legal* questions I ask you meaningless but so, too, are those *inner* questions you ask yourselves meaningless. Failing one's, partner does *not* matter. Sexual disappointment does *not* matter. Sexual betrayal does *not* matter. Nothing can hurt if we do not see it as hurtful. Nothing can destroy unless we see it as destructive. It is all part of life. Part of what we are. So, now, Alfred. Do you take Patricia as your lawfully wedded wife, to love—whatever *that* means—to honor—but is not dishonor, in a sense, a *form* of honor?— to keep her in sickness, in health, in prosperity and adversity—what nonsense!—forsaking all others—what a shocking invasion of privacy! Rephrase that to more sensibly say: if you *choose* to have affairs you won't feel guilty about them—as long as you both shall live—or as long as you're not bored of one another?

ALFRED. (*Numb.*) I do.

DUPAS. So. Patricia. Do you take Alfred, here, as your lawfully wedded husband to love—that harmful word— can't we more wisely say: communicate?—to honor—

meaning, I suppose, you won't cut his balls off; yet some men like that—and to obey—well, my very first look at you told me you were not the type to obey, so I went through the thesaurus and came up with these alternatives: to be loyal, to show fealty, to show devotion, to answer the helm, to be pliant—general enough, I would think, and still leave plenty of room to dominate—in sickness, in health and all the rest of that gobbledegook as long as you both shall live?

PATSY. (*Struggling to suppress her fury.*) I do.

DUPAS. Alfred and Patsy. I know now that whatever you do will be all right. And Patsy's father, Carol Newquist—I've never heard that name on a man before, but I'm sure it's all right— I ask you, sir, not to feel guilt over the two hundred and fifty dollar check you gave me to mention the Deity in this ceremony. What you have done is all right. It is part of what you are, what we all are. And I beg you not to be overly perturbed when I do not mention the Deity in this ceremony. Betrayal, too, is all right. It is part of what we all are. And Patsy's brother, Kenneth Newquist, in whose bedroom I spent a few moments earlier this afternoon and whose mother proudly told me the decoration was by your hand *entirely:* I beg of you to feel no shame; homosexuality is all right—

(KENNY *and* CAROL, *followed by* MARJORIE *and* GUESTS, *charge* DUPAS. *Outraged screams and cries as they mob and beat him.* PATSY *staggers off.* CAROL *turns on* ALFRED, *who is lost in a daze, and begins to slug away at him.* ALFRED *stands unflinching as:*)

CURTAIN SLOWLY FALLS

ACT TWO

SCENE 1

Four hours later. The Newquist apartment is strewn with wedding litter. ALFRED *and* CAROL *have not moved since last scene. They stand in half dark,* CAROL *sluggishly pounding away at* ALFRED, *who is obviously in a dream world. PHONE rings several times.* PATSY *enters, answers phone. Amplified BREATHING.*

PATSY. (*Into phone.*) You're all we need today. (*Hangs up. To* CAROL.) Daddy, you've been at it for hours. Will you please come away from there? (*She helps* CAROL *off.* ALFRED *doesn't move. She re-enters, stares a long while at him.*) Mother's hysterical, Daddy's collapsed and Kenny's disappeared with my wardrobe. I hope you're pleased with your day's work. (*She goes to him.*) You can stop daydreaming, Alfred. Nobody's hitting . . .

(*Stops. Takes off wedding glove. Cocks back fist. Holds, undecided.*)

ALFRED. (*Coming out of trance.*) I thought it was a very nice ceremony. (*She drops fist.*) A little hokey—

PATSY. (*Controlling herself.*) Alfred? (*Waves hand in front of his face.*) What's going to become of us if you go on this way? Weren't you *there?* Weren't you *listening?* I wanted a wedding! What in God's name do you use for feelings?

ALFRED. I feel.

PATSY. You don't feel.

ALFRED. Have it your way.

PATSY. There you go again! You won't fight!

ALFRED. You knew I wouldn't fight before you married me. I didn't realize it was a prerequisite.

PATSY. Well, maybe it is. More and more I think it is. If you don't fight you don't feel. If you don't feel you don't love.

ALFRED. I don't know— (*Together with* PATSY.) what love is.

PATSY. Of course you don't know! Because you don't feel.

ALFRED. I feel what I want to feel.

PATSY. (*An impulsive kiss.*) It's like kissing white bread. You don't feel. Alfred, what is it with you? It gets worse instead of better! I've never had a man do this to me before. It's not just pain you don't feel, you don't feel *pleasure!*

ALFRED. I do feel pleasure.

PATSY. About what?

ALFRED. A lot of things.

PATSY. Name one.

ALFRED. (*Pause.*) My work.

PATSY. Name another.

ALFRED. (*Pause.*) Sleeping.

PATSY. Work and sleeping! That's just great! What about sex?

ALFRED. (*Pause.*) It helps you sleep better.

PATSY. Alfred, do you mean half the things you say? You *must* feel something! (*No response. She snaps her fingers in his face. No response. She holds her head.*) Jesus Christ! (*Very tired.*) Alfred, why did you marry me?

ALFRED. You're comfortable.

PATSY. *I've never made men comfortable!* I'm popular because I make them uncertain! *You don't understand the first thing about me!*

ALFRED. Patsy, you're screaming.

PATSY. *Screaming! You son of a bitch, I'll tear you limb from limb! I married you because I wanted to mold*

*you. I loved the man I wanted to mold you into. But
you're not even there! How can I mold you if you're not
there?*

ALFRED. Everything I say makes you unhappy. We
used to get along so well—

PATSY. Because I did all the talking! My God! That's
why you were always so quiet. You weren't listening!

ALFRED. Sure I was.

PATSY. Don't lie, Alfred. I used to stare into those eyes
of yours, so warm, so complete with understanding—and
now I remember where I've seen those eyes since—when
my father was hitting you! *That's* the way you look when
you're daydreaming!

ALFRED. You don't get hurt that way.

PATSY. Honey, I don't want to hurt you. I want to
change you. I want to save you. I want to make you see
that there is some value in life, that there is some beauty,
some tenderness, some things worth reacting to. Some
things *worth* feeling— (*Snaps fingers in front of his
eyes.*) Come back here! I swear, Alfred, *nobody* is going
to kill you. But you've got to take some *chances* some-
time! What do you want out of life? Just *survival?*

ALFRED. (*Nods.*) And to take pictures.

PATSY. Of shit?! It's not enough! It's not, not, not
enough! I'm not going to have a surviving marriage, I'm
going to have a flourishing marriage! I'm a *woman!* Or,
by Jesus, it's about time I became one. I want a family!
Oh, Christ, Alfred, this is my wedding day— (*Pause.
Regains composure.*) I want— I want to be married to
a big, strong, protective, vital, virile, self-assured man.
Who I can protect and take care of. Alfred, honey, you're
the first man I've ever gone to bed with where I didn't
feel *he* was a lot more likely to get pregnant than I was.
(*Desperate.*) You owe me something! I've invested everything I believe in you. You've *got* to let me mold you.
Please let me mold you. (*Regains control.*) You've got
me begging. You're got me whining, begging and crying.
I've never behaved like this in my life. Will you look at

this? (*Holds out finger.*) That's a tear. I never cried in my life.

ALFRED. Me neither.

PATSY. You never cried because you were too terrified of everything to let yourself *feel!* You'd have to learn crying from a manual! Chop onions! I never cried because I was too tough—but I felt *everything.* Every slight, every pressure, every vague competition—but I *fought.* And I *won!* There hasn't been a battle since I was five that I haven't won! And the people I fought were happy that I won! *Happy!* After a while, Alfred, do you have any idea how many people in this town *worship* me? Maybe that's the attraction—you don't worship me. (*Shakes head.*) Maybe I'd lose all respect for you if you did all the things I want you to do. (*Thinks on it.*) Alfred, *you've got* to change! (*Regains calm.*) Listen. (*Pause.*) I'm not saying I'm better or stronger than you are. It's just that we—you and I—have different temperaments. (*Explodes.*) *And my temperament is better and stronger than yours!* (*Frantic.*) You're a *wall!* (*Circles him.*) You don't fight! You hardly ever listen! Dear God, will somebody please explain to me why I think you're so beautiful. (*PHONE rings. She picks it up. Amplified BREATHING.*) *Leave me alone! What do you want out of me? Will you please leave me alone?*

(ALFRED, *shocked by outburst, takes phone away.*)

ALFRED. (*Into phone.*) She can't talk now.

(*Hangs up. Takes* PATSY, *sobbing violently, in his arms.*)

PATSY. (*Empty.*) Alfred, it's all shit. How come I never noticed before?

ALFRED. Patsy—

PATSY. You were right. I'm just dense. *I'm* the one who doesn't feel. It's all terrible . . . terrible . . . terrible.

ALFRED. Come on, Patsy.

PATSY. No more reason for *anything*.

ALFRED. (*Uncomfortable. Weakly.*) Mrs. Newquist!

PATSY. The only true feeling is no feeling. The only way to survive. You're one hundred percent right. Hold my hand. (ALFRED *backs away.*) I'm sorry. I'm not this weak, really. You know how tough I am. I'll be just as tough again. I promise. I just have to learn to be tough about shit. And I will. (ALFRED *backs off to a chair.*)

ALFRED. I feel weak.

PATSY. Alfred, we can't both feel weak at the same time.

ALFRED. (*An admission.*) Patsy, you're beginning to get me nervous. You have to listen to me for a minute—

PATSY. You're right. I'm wrong. Everything is the way you say. (*Begins to withdraw.*) You sit. (*Sits.*) You get old. (*Freezes.*) You die.

(*Stares as if in one of* ALFRED's *daydreams.* ALFRED *goes to her. Touches her head. No reaction. Lifts her to standing position. She slides back down. He stares at her, horrified, then goes into his daydream stare. He slides into the chair opposite hers.* BOTH *stare blankly into space.* PHONE *rings. Many rings.* ALFRED *finally rises, crosses to phone, numbly lifts it. Amplified BREATHING.*)

ALFRED. Thanks. I'm up. (*Hangs up. Stares thoughtfully at* PATSY.) During Korea—I was in college then —the government couldn't decide whether I was a security risk or not— I wore a beard—so they put a mail check on me. Every day the mail would come later and later. And it would be bent. Corners torn. Never sealed correctly. Like they didn't give a damn whether I knew they were reading my mail or not. I was more of a militant in those days, so I decided to fight fire with fire. I began writing letters to the guy who was reading my mail. I addressed them to myself, of course, but inside they went something like: "Dear Sir: I am not that different from you. All men are brothers. Tomorrow instead of reading my mail in that dark, dusty hall why not bring it upstairs where we can check it out together!" I never got an answer. So I wrote a second letter. "Dear Sir: There are no heroes, no villains, no good guys, no bad guys. The world is more complicated than that. Come on up where we can open a couple of beers and talk it all out." (*Checks* PATSY. *No reaction.*) Again, no answer. So then I wrote: "Dear Sir: I've been thinking too much of my own problems, too little of yours. Yours cannot be a happy task—reading another man's mail. It's dull, unimaginative. A job—and let's not mince words—for a hack. Yet I wonder—can this be the way you see yourself? Do you see yourself as a hack? Do you see yourself as the office slob? Have you ever *wondered* why they stuck you with this particular job, instead of others who have *less* seniority? Or, was it, do you think, that your supervisor looked around the office to see who he'd stick for the job, saw *you* and said, 'No one will miss *him* for a month!'" And still, no answer. But *that* letter— (*Checks* PATSY.) that letter never got delivered to me. So *then* I wrote: "Dear Friend: Just a note to advise: you may retain my letters as long as you deem fit. Reread them. Study them. Think them out. Who back at the office is *out to get you?* Who, at this *very* moment, is sitting at *your* desk, reading *your* mail? I do not say this to be cruel, but because I am the only one left you can *trust*—" No answer. *But*—the next day a man, saying he was from the telephone company showed up—no complaint had been made—to check the phone. Shaky hands.

Bloodshot eyes. A small quaver in his voice. And as he dismembered my phone he said, "Look. What nobody understands is that everybody has his job to do. I got my job. In this case it's repairing telephones. I like it or I don't like it but it's my job. If I had another job— say, for example, with the F.B.I.—or someplace, putting in a wiretap, for example, or reading a guy's mail—*like it or don't like it it would be my job!* Has anyone got the right to *destroy* a man for doing his job?" I wrote one more letter—expressing my deep satisfaction that he and I had at last made contact, and informing him that the next time he came, perhaps to read the meter, I had valuable information, photostats, recordings, names and dates, about the conspiracy against him. This letter showed up a week after I mailed it, in a crumpled grease-stained, and scotch-taped envelope. The letter itself was torn in half and then clumsily glued together again. In the margin, on the bottom, in large, shaky letters was written the word "Please!" I wasn't bothered again. It was after this that I began to wonder: If they're *that* un-formidable why bother to fight back? (PATSY *moves.*) It's very dangerous to challenge a system unless you're completely at peace with the thought that you're not going to miss it when it collapses. (PATSY, *faltering, rises, with* ALFRED'S *help, to her feet.*) Patsy—you can't be the one to change. (PATSY *stares, uncomprehending.*) I'm the one who has to change.

PATSY. (*Tired.*) Alfred, what are you talking about?

ALFRED. When I first met you I remember thinking: this is the most formidable person I have ever known. I don't stand a *chance!* I'll try to stay the way I am. I'll try *desperately!* (*Happily.*) *But I don't stand a chance!* It's only a matter of time. Very soon now I'll be— (*Smiles.*) *different.* I'll be able to look at half empty glasses of water—and say: "This glass isn't half empty. This glass is half full!" *You* can't be the one to sell out. *I* was supposed to sell out. (*Stares miserably at the di-sheveled, slumped over* PATSY *he's created. Puts fingers to his head.*) Why doesn't somebody beat me up now? (*Starts off.*) I'm going out to Central Park! (*Exits.*)

PATSY. (*Watches him go. Slowly straightens.*) Alfred— *Come back here!* You see what happens when you start fooling around with the rules? (*Recovering, holds out her arms.*) It begins with weddings and it ends with—well, there's no telling where it ends. There are reasons for doing things the old way. Don't look for trouble and trouble won't look for you. (*With growing assurance.*) I don't say there aren't problems but you have to fight. You are going to fight. (*Squeezes arms around him.*) Starting now. Is that right? (*Pause. Finally he nods.*) And you are going to feel. Starting right now. Is that right? (*Long pause. He nods.*) I don't want a nod. I want an answer. Say, "Yes, Patsy."

ALFRED. Yes, Patsy.

PATSY. Yes, Patsy, what?

ALFRED. Yes, Patsy—I'm going to feel.

PATSY. Starting when?

ALFRED. Starting as soon as I can manage it.

PATSY. Starting *when?*

ALFRED. Starting now.

PATSY. And what's your first feeling?

ALFRED. It's sort of distant.

PATSY. Don't be ashamed of it.

ALFRED. It's worship.

PATSY. Of God?

ALFRED. Of you.

PATSY. You're doing fine. (*Kisses him. Puts her arms round him.*) My lover. (*Kisses him.*) My hero!

(*Kisses him.* ALFRED *tentatively responds. Embrace builds.* CAROL *and* MARJORIE *enter. React with warm surprise. They put their arms around each other.*)

MARJORIE. Aren't they an attractive couple?

(Sound of a GUNSHOT. WINDOW shatters. Explosion of BLOOD as PATSY'S *hand flies up to her head. She drops.* CAROL *and* MARJORIE *freeze.* ALFRED *stares down at* PATSY, *then melts, slowly, into his day-dream pose. The STREET NOISE is loud through the shattered window.)*

BLACKOUT

ACT TWO

SCENE 2

The Newquist apartment. Six months later. There have been changes. Heavy blackout drapes cover the windows. Large photographic blow-ups of Patsy's eyes, nose, hair, smiling lips, and teeth are hung, unframed, on the wall, and are in evidence in several two and three foot high stacks on the floor. ALFRED *is bent over a small photo stand, shooting away with a camera, humming to himself. He looks happy. Sporadic GUNFIRE is heard in the background. He pays no attention. DOORBELL.* ALFRED *takes a quick last look at the work on the stand, goes to the door, detouring past couch to push out of sight the protruding edge of a long cardboard carton. He has the beginnings of a black eye.*

ALFRED. One minute. (*He checks through keyhole and unlocks door. There are now four different kinds of locks and bolts on the door including a police bar.*) One more minute. (*Opens door.*) Hi, Dad!

CAROL. (*Enters carrying bulging brief case.*) It's murder out there.

ALFRED. Hey, Dad, you're limping.

CAROL. (*Shouts.*) *How many times have I told you not to call me Dad!*

ALFRED. I can't call you "Dad." I can't call you "Carol." What can I call you? "Dear?"

(*Long exchange of stares,* ALFRED'S *good-humored,* CAROL'S *sullen.*)

CAROL. Call me Mr. Newquist.

ALFRED. Oh, come on, Dad, you're just in a bad mood. Let me fix you a drink. (*Crosses to bar.*)

CAROL. (*Sits.*) I don't want you to fix me— Bourbon.

ALFRED. (*Serving drink.*) The family that drinks together sinks together.

CAROL. Maybe I'd feel better if you turned on the air conditioner. It blots out the sound of the shooting. Agh, the hell with it. It's here to stay. I might as well get used to it. (*Conspiratorial.*) I dropped by police headquarters this afternoon. That's why I'm late.

ALFRED. Are you late?

CAROL. (*Annoyed.*) *Yes, I'm late!* I'm four hours late. I told you I'd be finished with my deliveries at one. Any calls?

ALFRED. The breather, once or twice. He's picking up the pace again.

CAROL. (*Mutters.*) Asthmatic bastard!

ALFRED. I never told you, but the day after Patsy died he rang up. I went a little crazy— I started screaming, "Didn't you hear the news? No need to call any more! Patsy's dead!" In no more than ten seconds—he called back. And he *spoke!* He said, "I don't know what to say. I'm terribly sorry." And then before hanging up he said, "What can we do? The world's gone crazy!" Not another breath out of him until this week. In mourning, I suppose.

CAROL. You sure it's the same one?

ALFRED. You think we're on a mailing list? God, I *hope* it's the same one.

CAROL. This damned business! (*Conspiratorial.*) Keep

this under your hat—but I paid an unexpected call on police headquarters this afternoon.

ALFRED. I'm surprised they didn't shoot you.

CAROL. They did shoot me. (*Rubs leg.*) It was my own damned fault. I didn't give the password. I feel sorry for those poor bastards. I know a lot of them by their first names. I call them Jimmy, and Mac, and Phil. They call me Carol. (*Quickly.*) It sounds different when they say it. Three hundred and forty-five unsolved murders in the last six months. Poor bastards are going crazy. I had a fifteen-minute talk with Lieutenant Practice. Busy as hell, but he found fifteen minutes to talk to me. He's convinced they're closing in on the conspiracy.

ALFRED. What conspiracy?

CAROL. Three hundred and forty-five unsolved murders in six months. There's got to be a conspiracy. There's got to be some logic behind all this. Any other calls?

ALFRED. You mean orders? No.

CAROL. I'm surprised. I have to admit to you these new pictures are really catching on! Fifty orders of Patsy number one last week, ten orders so far this week of Patsy number five and fifteen, and five orders from an uptown gallery for the entire Patsy series. (*Thickly.*) We wouldn't have come through this without you, Alfred.

ALFRED. (*Shrugs.*) I had to do *something* after I abandoned my shit series.

CAROL. (*Emotional.*) But you didn't have to put *me* to work. Nobody asked— (*Suddenly defensive.*) *I* didn't ask—

ALFRED. You're a top-notch salesman, Dad.

CAROL. Don't kid. I hate being kidded. I'm an order taker and a messenger boy. But when I get back on my feet—

ALFRED. It'll be no time.

CAROL. It should've been long before this. Who knows if they'll even want me back at the office? Six months— (*Shakes head.*) You've been very good to us.

ALFRED. Forget it.

CAROL. (*Nods.*) I'll do that. (*A pained sigh.*) I wish I resented you less.

ALFRED. Keep up the fight, tiger.

CAROL. (*Sadly.*) Patsy used to call me tiger. Everything you say, these days, reminds me of Patsy.

ALFRED. (*Thoughtful, a little sad.*) I owe Patsy a lot. (*Cheerful again.*) Why shouldn't I talk like her?

CAROL. Just as long as you don't dress like her. Where's Kenny?

ALFRED. In her closet.

CAROL. Little son of a bitch. Christ, I hope it's only a phase. I don't see where that Doctor Harm is helping him any.

ALFRED. Doctor Good.

CAROL. Yeah? Well, I suppose he must be good. Otherwise he'd take a hell of a kidding. (*Depressed.*) Agh—I don't understand anything anymore. You know how I get through the day? In planned segments. I get up in the morning and I think: Okay, a sniper didn't get me for breakfast, let's see if I can go for my morning walk without being mugged. Okay, I finished my walk, let's see if I can make it back home without having a brick dropped on my head from the top of a building. Okay, I'm safe in the lobby, let's see if I can go up in the elevator without getting a knife in my ribs. Okay, I made it to the front door, let's see if I can open it without finding burglars in the living room. Okay, I made it to the living room, let's see if I can walk into the bedroom and not find the rest of my family dead. This God-damned city!

ALFRED. Got to fight, tiger.

CAROL. You do enough fighting for one family. Where'd you get that eye?

ALFRED. Some kid was staring at me in the park. I hit him.

CAROL. Another fight?

ALFRED. What could I do? The little bastard was staring at me! (CAROL *turns away in disgust.*) I beat the crap out of him— (CAROL *reluctantly smiles*. ALFRED *starts to spar with him*.) Let's go a couple of quick ones, tiger!—

CAROL. (*Retreating*.) Come on. Cut it out. Cut it out.

ALFRED. Pow! Pow! Pow! Boy, if Patsy could only have been there! And she said I didn't feel. Every time I get into one of these things, I think of her— I think of her alive and me coming home weary, every night—you know, after I beat somebody up, and she meets me at the door, looking up at me with eyes full of pride, and she takes my swollen fists in her hands and she kisses my knuckles. What a dream. Why is it we only learn when it's too late? It was my fourth fight this week. Anyhow, I got very faint. I suppose all that euphoria takes something out of you, so I sat down on a park bench to rest—and I found *this* lying there.

(*Holds up* Daily News.)

CAROL. (*Reading*.) "Hippie Minister Slain at Church Happening." They're sure giving that son of a bitch a hell of a lot of free publicity.

ALFRED. It wasn't so much the story that interested me. I don't have the patience for facts, or any of that nonsense any more. What interested me was— (*Shows* CAROL *newspaper*.) This photograph of the body— What does it look like?

CAROL. That son of a bitch. With his eyes closed.

ALFRED. (*Excited*.) No! Look closer!

CAROL. What do I want to look for? This is the silliest—

ALFRED. Don't you see the dots?

CAROL. What dots?

ALFRED. Here! The little black dots that make up the photograph. Use your eyes, Dad.

CAROL. Okay, I see them! So what!

ALFRED. Keep staring at them. You see how they slowly begin to move? (*Takes paper away from* CAROL.) I was sitting on the park bench—looking at this photograph of the body—and the little black dots began to break apart—they began detaching themselves from the body—the dots that make up the eyes—the little black dots that make up his mouth—and the top of his head—they just lifted off Henry's body—and broke apart. Until it wasn't the body of Henry Dupas I was staring at but millions of little black dots—coming at me until I thought I was going to be sucked in alive. I panicked! I began to close off! But then I thought: Wait a minute.— That's the old you; the pre-Patsy you. So I let go and I was swallowed. Into a free-floating constellation of dots. Fantastic! I swung my eyes away from the photograph—I looked up at a tree. Do you know how many trillions of dots there are in one Central Park tree? And then the dots that made up the tree merged with the dots that made up the sky—merged with the dots that made up the park bench and the grass and the dirt path and the three colored kids walking toward me carrying bicycle chains. Do you know the wild arrangement of dots that's made every time you punch somebody out? Those poor kids must have thought I was crazy—humming as I beat their heads against the sidewalk. I've been studying this newspaper for hours now, trying to figure out a way of decomposing everything into dots.

CAROL. I don't know why you want to fool around. We're doing *extremely* well with our current line.

ALFRED. There gets to be something ultimately stifling about taking photographs of old photographs.

CAROL. (*Reasonably.*) You enlarge them.

ALFRED. It's so limited. I want to do *life!* If I could somehow make people see themselves as trillions upon trillions of free-wheeling, interchanging dots— (*DOOR-BELL. Goes to door.*) One minute. (*Looks through peep-hole. Begins process of unlocking door.*) One more minute.

(MARJORIE *enters, flushed, carrying leaking shopping bag.*)

MARJORIE. Will you look at this mess? They shot a hole in my shopping bag.

CAROL. You could have been killed!

MARJORIE. (*Annoyed.*) I get shot at every day. We all do, Carol. Don't make any more of it than it is. (*To* ALFRED.) I saw that nice Lieutenant Practice in the lobby. He looks simply awful. I invited him up for coffee just as soon as he gets finished investigating the new murder.

CAROL. What new murder?

MARJORIE. I don't know. It's in the other wing.

(CAROL *evades her stare.* ALFRED *reaches under couch and slides out two boxes. The long one he pushes back under, the smaller one he hands to* MARJORIE.)

ALFRED. Mom.

MARJORIE. (*Opens box.*) Alfred. Oh, Alfred! (*Removes flowers.*) Look, Carol, they're flowers! (*Clutches them to her. Cries.*) I'm sorry—there is so little thought left of giving today that I've forgotten how to receive. (*Drops flowers. Rushes off, holding hands to face. Offstage.*) Kenny! Let me in there!

(*Offstage toilet FLUSH.* KENNY *comes in carrying* Vogue. CAROL, *who cannot look at him, exits.* KENNY *sees flowers, picks them up.*)

ALFRED. You want 'em?

KENNY. (*Drops flowers.*) What do I want with your fruity flowers?

MARJORIE. (*Enters, stares down at flowers.*) Aren't they beautiful? When I was twelve and a half my mother and father would always cart the whole pack of us out to the country—and we would always picnic near the flowers. There were so many more flowers in those days. We would pick every last one and bring it back to the city. (*Door CHIMES. KENNY starts for door.*) You better let me get it. (KENNY *strides over to window.*) Who is it? Will you step a little closer and turn your face into the light please?

(*She checks peephole, starts to unlock door. KENNY, at window, parts drapes and stares out.*)

ALFRED. (*Still peering into camera on stand.*) That's—not—a—good—idea—

KENNY. (*Whirls.*) Who died and made you boss? (*SHOT splinters pane above KENNY's head just as LIEUTENANT PRACTICE enters. Shakes fist and screams.*) Fags!

MARJORIE. (*To PRACTICE.*) You'll have to pardon the mess.

(CAROL *enters, glances over to KENNY at window, hurries over to PRACTICE, shakes his hand.*)

CAROL. Well, well, well. This is an unexpected pleasure. Alfred, look who's decided to pay us a visit. Lieutenant Practice! (ALFRED, *at work, gives perfunctory wave of hand. Whispers.*) He's working. Goes on day and night. It's no accident he's successful.

PRACTICE. And I'm not. Is that it?

CAROL. (*Takes his arm.*) I didn't mean that. You people have got to stop being over-sensitive. You're making great strides. Nobody expects very much, anyway. (PRACTICE *draws arm away.*) Nobody's complaining.

MARJORIE. (*Cheerful.*) We certainly haven't complained. And if anyone has a right to—

PRACTICE. (*Sad.*) Can I please have a glass of milk, Mrs. Newquist?

MARJORIE. Of course, dear.

PRACTICE. And a cookie. Jeez, I'm depressed. There's got to be some logical explanation to all of this.

(MARJORIE *exits.*)

CAROL. You've got nothing to be ashamed of. You'll figure it out.

PRACTICE. (*Hands* CAROL *envelope.*) I really stopped by to return this. I don't know what got into me this afternoon.

CAROL. (*Looks nervously around.*) It's all right. It's yours! Forget it!

PRACTICE. I *can't* accept a two hundred and fifty dollar check. I know your heart was in the right place, Mr. Newquist, but believe me, it's not gonna make us find your daughter's murderer any quicker.

CAROL. Keep it! Keep it! You never can tell—

MARJORIE. (*Enters with glass of milk.*) Drink this. You'll feel better. Carol, are you giving money away again? You know, Lieutenant, every time we pass a policeman he hands him five dollars.

CAROL. I just want the boys on the beat to know somebody still has faith in them.

PRACTICE. (*Drinks.*) I needed this. (*Examines hand holding glass. It has a tremor.*) I wasn't like this when I met you six months ago, was I? Wasn't I a lot more self-confident? Jeez, the way I used to enter the scene of a crime! Like I owned the God-damned world! Can you put a little scotch in this milk, please? And a piece of cheese on this cookie? There's going to be a shakeup, you know. When there are three hundred and forty-five murders and none of them get solved— (*Angry.*) *somebody has to be elected fall guy!* (*Accepts drink.*) Thank you. Maybe a piece of ice like a good fellow. (*Hands drink back.*) Somewhere there's a logical pattern to this whole business. There *has* to be. (*Accepts cookie.*) Thank you. And these damned vigilante groups—they're not helping matters. Black against white. White against black. Whatever became of human dignity? (*Accepts drink.*) Oh, for Christ sakes, only *one* piece of ice? Let's get it right, huh? Say, what kind of cheese is this? Sharp cheddar? You ought to know by now with my stomach I can't take sharp cheddar! Come on! *Will you shape up?* (*Reflective.*) Sooner or later there's a pattern. Sooner or later everything falls into place. I believe that. If I didn't believe that I wouldn't want to wake up to see the sun tomorrow morning. (CAROL *and* MARJORIE *scrambling from different directions with drink and cheese.*) Is *this* what I asked for? God damn it, I want *some cooperation!* (*A SHOT. Milk GLASS explodes in his hand.* ALL *except* PRACTICE *stare toward window. He stares at remnant of glass in his hand.*) Every crime has its own pattern of logic. Everything has an order. If we can't find that order it's not because it doesn't exist but only because we've incorrectly observed some vital piece of evidence. Let us examine the evidence. (*Places glass in handkerchief in pocket.*) Number one. In the last six months, three hundred and forty-five homicides have been committed in this city. The victims have ranged variously in sex, age, social status and color. Number two. In none of the three hundred and forty-five homicides have we been able to establish motive. Number three. All three hundred and forty-five homicides remain listed on our books as unsolved. So much for the evidence. A subtle pattern begins to emerge.

What is this pattern? What is it that each of these three
hundred and forty-five homicides have in common? They
have in common three things: A—that they have nothing
in common; B—that they have no motive; C—that, con-
sequently, they remain unsolved. The pattern becomes
clearer. Orthodox police procedure dictates that the basic
questions you ask in all such investigations is one: Who
has the most to gain? What could possibly be the single
unifying motive behind three hundred and forty-five un-
connected homicides? When a case does not jell it is
often not because we lack the necessary facts, but because
we have observed our facts incorrectly. In each of these
three hundred and forty-five homicides we observed our
facts incorrectly. Following normal routine we looked for a
cause. And we could find no cause. Had we looked for
effect we would have had our answer that much sooner.
What is the effect of three hundred and forty-five unsolved homicide cases? The effect is loss of faith in law-
enforcement personnel. That is our motive. The pattern
is complete. We are involved here in a far-reaching conspiracy to undermine respect for our basic beliefs and
most sacred institutions. Who is behind this conspiracy?
Once again ask the question: who has the most to gain?
People in high places. Their names would astound you.
People in low places. Concealing their activities beneath a
cloak of poverty. People in all walks of life. Left wing
and right wing. Black and white. Students and scholars. A
conspiracy of such ominous proportions that we may not
know the whole truth in our lifetime and we will never
be able to reveal all the facts. We are readying mass
arrests. (*Rises to leave.*) I'm going to try my best to see
that you people get every possible break. If there is any
information you wish to volunteer at this time it will be
held in the strictest confidence. (*Waits for response. There
is none. Crosses to door and opens it.*) I strongly advise
against any of you trying to leave town. (*Quick exit.*)

CAROL. (*Gradually exploding.*) What's left? What's
there left? I'm a resonable man. Just explain to me what I

have left to believe in. I swear to God the tide's rising! Two hundred and fifty dollars. Gimme. Gimme. We need honest cops. People just aren't being protected any more. We need a revival of honor. And trust. We need the army. We need a giant fence around every block in the city. An electrically charged fence. And anyone who wants to leave the block has to have a pass. And a haircut. And can't talk with a filthy mouth. We need respect for a man's reputation. T.V. cameras. That's what we need. In every building lobby, in every elevator, in every apartment, in every room. Public servants who are public servants. And if they catch you doing anything funny—to yourself—or anybody—they break down the door and beat the living— A return to common sense. We have to have lobotomies for anyone who earns less than ten thousand a year. I don't like it, but it's an emergency. Our side needs weapons too. Is it fair that they should have all the weapons? We've got to train ourselves. And steel ourselves. It's freedom I'm talking about! There's a fox loose in the chicken coop. Kill him! I want my freedom! (*Collapses.*)

(ALFRED *and* MARJORIE *carry* CAROL *off.* KENNY *watches after them, accidentally kicks foot against large box under couch. Notices it for the first time. Slides it out. Opens it. Takes out rifle. Quickly hides rifle as* MARJORIE *enters, crosses to bathroom, returns with towel and exits.* KENNY *picks up rifle, goes to window, parts curtains slightly, aims.* ALFRED *enters.* KENNY, *startled, holds rifle out to him.*)

KENNY. I thought it was more flowers.
ALFRED. Use it.
KENNY. What do I want to use it for? I've only been in analysis for four months. I've never fired one of these in my life.
ALFRED. Me too.
KENNY. (*Suspicious.*) Why'd you get it?

ALFRED. (*Shrugs.*) It was on sale. Put it away—
(KENNY *begins to.*) No— (ALFRED *crosses to* KENNY, *takes rifle, studies it.*) You notice, if you stare at it long enough it breaks into dots?

KENNY. (*Studies rifle.*) No—

ALFRED. (*Turns rifle in hand.*) Trillions of dots. (*Pulls trigger. A loud click.*) It's not loaded. (*Puts it down.*)

KENNY. Why don't you load it?

ALFRED. I don't know how. (*Hands rifle to* KENNY *who backs away from it.*)

KENNY. (*Shakes head.*) The army rejected me four times. The fifth time they said if I ever come around again they'd have me arrested. (*Reaches into box.*) Here's an instruction booklet. (*Reads.*) "Nomenclature. Trigger Housing Group. To load. Hold the weapon by the forearm of the stock. With the left hand rotate the safety catch to its 'off' position. With the right hand retract the bolt and insert the ammunition clip. . . ."

(ALFRED *with great deliberateness and considerable difficulty tries to follow the instructions.*)

MARJORIE. (*Enters. Looks over* ALFRED'S *shoulder.*) I don't know about these things, dear, but I found the best way to deal with the unfamiliar is to think things back to their source. (*She takes rifle out of his hands.*) Now, it would seem to me that *this* goes in— (*Struggles.* CAROL *enters. Observes.*) Damn it! They must have given you the wrong— (CAROL *takes rifle out of her hands, expertly loads it, tosses it to* ALFRED. *Very impressed.*) *Dear!*

ALFRED. (*Hands rifle back to* CAROL.) Go on, Dad. You loaded it. You go first.

CAROL. (*Solemnly hands rifle back.*) It's yours.

KENNY. Where'd you learn that, Dad? It's a trick, right?

(CAROL *stares scornfully at* KENNY, *takes rifle.* ALFRED *parts curtains.*)

ALFRED. Can you see well enough?

(CAROL *aims, fires.*)

KENNY. You got somebody.
MARJORIE. Let me see! I never can see! Yes! Yes! Somebody's lying there!
CAROL. (*To* ALFRED.) Why don't you try *your* luck? (*Hands over rifle.*)
ALFRED. (*Hands rifle to* KENNY.) You first, Kenny.
KENNY. Gee.
ALFRED. (*Reassuring.*) I'll go right after you.

(KENNY *quickly up with rifle. Fires out of window.*)

CAROL. Miss!
KENNY. You made me nervous! You were *looking!*
CAROL. (*Takes rifle.*) It's Alfred's turn.
KENNY. No fair. You shook my arm.
ALFRED. Let him have another shot.

(KENNY *aims carefully, fires.*)

CAROL. (*Looking into street. Very proud.*) Son of a bitch!
MARJORIE. (*Hugs him.*) You did it! You did it!

(CAROL *reloads. Hands rifle to* ALFRED.)

KENNY. (*Cool.*) Dad and I got *our* two.

(CAROL *puts his arm round* KENNY'S *shoulder.* ALFRED *aims out of the window, fires.*)

CAROL. You know who I think he got?
MARJORIE. Lieutenant Practice! (ALL *jump up and*

down in self-congratulations. Ad-lib. shouts, Texas yells.
MARJORIE *detaches herself, exits to come back wheeling*
a serving cart. She lights candles on dining table.) Come
an' git it! (*Others, wrestling, horsing around move slowly*
toward table.) Boys!

(*Amidst great noise, bustle, serving of drinks, they finally*
    sit. Many pointed fingers, ad-lib. cries of "Beginner's
    luck!" friendly shoving.)

ALFRED. Hey, how about Mom trying her luck after
dinner?

(*Cheers, ad-lib. agreement.*)

MARJORIE. (*Serving.*) It's so nice to have my family
laughing again. You know for a while I was really worried.

(*General merriment.*)

CURTAIN

PROPS SETTING LIST

ACT I—*Scene 1*

SET:

On D. R. Drinks Cabinet:
  8 highball glasses
  Ice thermidor with ice
  2 bottles tonic water
  2 bottles Canada Dry
  Bottle opener
  CLOSE DRINKS CABINET

D. L. of Drinks Cabinet:
  Cardboard carton containing:
  1 bottle Bourbon
  1 bottle Scotch Whiskey
  1 bottle Rye
  1 bottle Vodka

In U. S. compartment of Dining Table:
  Pair high heels

On Magazine Table:
  Magazines

On U. S. L. Table:
  Table lamp
  Ashtray

On D. L. Phone Table:
  Telephone
  Ashtray

Off Right (In Kitchen):
  Serving trolley containing:
  5 large forks
  5 small forks
  5 dessert spoons
  5 knives
  3 serving spoons
  8 table mats
  5 napkins
  1 ashtray
  Salt cellar
  Pepper pot

On Kitchen Prop Table:
  2 small dishes food
  1 large dish food
  5 wine glasses
  1 folded tablecloth
  1 damp sponge
  Small bottle with sprinkler top
  Pair oven gloves
  Bottle wine with cork and corkscrew
  Tea towel
  2 candlesticks

On Bedroom Prop Table:
  3 framed photographs
  Pair sunglasses
  Lace handkerchief
  Silk head scarf

Off Left—Prop Table:
  2 grocery bags with provisions
  Black brief case with documents
  2 camera cases
  Paperback
  Bunch of keys
  2 startling pistols—loaded
  .45 revolver—loaded
  Glass crash

Act I—*Scene 2*

Strike:
  Dining table top and contents
  Handbag from below table

From below Drinks Cabinet:
  Cardboard carton
  Empty wine bottle

From Drinks Cabinet:
  Vodka
  Old Grandad whiskey
  CLOSE DRINKS CABINET

From below Phone Table:
  Black brief case

Set for Act I—Scene 3:
  False table top containing:
  Champagne glasses
  3 bottles champagne
  Wedding cake
  Cables

Off Left—Prop Table:
  Rolaflex camera
  Camera in case and flash
  Basket of flowers
  Lens brush

Off Right—Prop Table:
  Check for DUPAS
  Basket of flowers

ACT II—*Scene 1*

STRIKE:
  Camera and flashgun

RE-SET in Drinks Cabinet:
  4 clean highball glasses
  Ice in thermidor
  Bottle Scotch—without top
  Bottle Bourbon—without top

SET:
Below P.S. window in corner:
  Golf club

ACT II—*Scene 2*

STRIKE:
  False table top

From O.P. hall:
  Basket of flowers

From Drinks Cabinet:
  Wedding dressing

Set Off Right for change:
  Photos
  Camera tripod with rolaflex and cord
  Music stand with 2 small photos

On Kitchen Prop Table:
  Breaking glass of milk
  2 small plates
  1 cookie
  1 cookie with butter and dark cheese
  1 cookie and dark cheese
  1 cookie and light cheese
  Dustpan and brush

On Bedroom Prop Table:
  Paperback

On Trolley in Kitchen:
  4 cans *opened* beans
  4 dessert spoons in bean cans
  4 cans Coca-cola
  1 can opener
  4 tin plates

Set Off Left for Change:
  6 Patsy photos
  Bundle plain cards
  Rifle in box
  Clip with ammo in rifle box
  Rifle instruction manual in rifle box
  Dummy bullets in clip in rifle box
  Flower box with flowers
  Large portfolio
  Dust cloth
  Leaking shopping bag
  Magnifying glass
  Square black card with hole
  Daily News—with insert

PERSONAL PROPS

PATSY:
  Pack of cigarettes and lighter

CAROL:
  Cigarette case with 6 cigarettes, spectacles, lighter, ballpoint pen, bandaid

ALFRED:
  Bandaid

RUNNING PLOT

Before the Half:
    CHECK:
- Air conditioner
- Furniture on marks
- Door—marie tempest
- Doorbell
- Windows
- Sliding window
- Crash box and hammer—outside P/S window
- 4 panes of glass
- Door slam O/P
- False table top
- U/S dining chair to step
- D/S window open
- Kitchen door—swinging
- Venetian blind
- Push U/S table to wall
- Drinks cabinet closed
- Projections
- Working lights out
- Masking
- Screen in

On Curtain Up—in Blackout:
    STAFF SET:
- Armchair
- Settee
- Telephone table

CHANGE—From Scene 1 to Scene 2:
    STRIKE:
- Brief case
- Tumblers
- Coats
- Candle lamp
- 2 cameras
- Table top
- Carton
- Handbag
- Shoes

Re-Set:
 Armchair
 Dining chairs
 Close drinks cabinet

CHANGE—From Scene 2 to Scene 3:
 Re-Set:
  Armchair
  Settee

 Set:
  2 baskets flowers
  Table top

END OF ACT ONE:
 In Blackout—Clear u. s.:
  Settee
  Armchair
  Magazine table
  Close door

INTERVAL:

 IRON IN:
 Set magazine table

 IRON OUT:
 Re-Set:
  Settee
  Armchair
  Dining table
  Dining chairs

 Set:
  2 piles of broken glass on crash box

ACT TWO

CHANGE—From Scene 1 to Scene 2:
 Strike:
  Table top
  2 baskets flowers
  1 dining chair
  Cushions
  Picture

RE-SET:
  Settee
  Curtains
  Armchair
  Magazine table

SET:
  Door plate
  Dust sheet—on settee
  Gun in box
  Flowers in box
  Camera and tripod
  B.O. curtain U./S. O./P.
  Venetian blind
  Music stand
  Photo flood
  Photographs
    Settee
    Carpet
    U. S. wall
    Kitchen wall
    O. P. arch
    D. S. O. P. wall
    Above door
  Pile of cards
  Magnifying glass

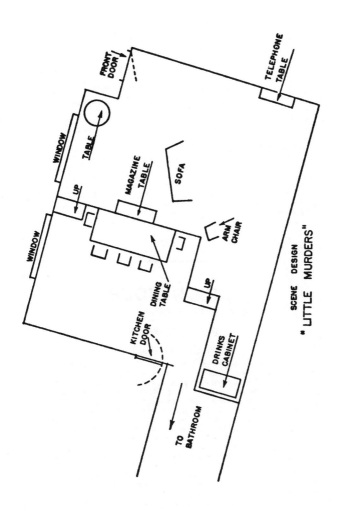

SCENE DESIGN
" LITTLE MURDERS"

FRONT DOOR

TELEPHONE TABLE

WINDOW

TABLE

MAGAZINE TABLE

SOFA

UP

WINDOW

ARM CHAIR

DINING TABLE

UP

KITCHEN DOOR

DRINKS CABINET

TO BATHROOM

71

Other Publications for Your Interest

GROWN UPS
(LITTLE THEATRE—COMEDY)
By JULES FEIFFER

2 men, 3 women, 1 female child—Interiors

An acerbic comedy by the famed cartoonist and author of *Knock Knock* and *Little Murders*. It's about a middle-aged journalist who has, at last, grown-up—only to find he's trapped in a world of emotional infants. "A laceratingly funny play about the strangest of human syndromes—the love that kills rather than comforts. Feiffer's vision seems merciless, but its mercy is the fierce comic clarity with which he exposes every conceivable permutation of smooth-tongued cruelty . . . Feiffer constructs a fiendishly complex machine of reciprocal irritation in which Jake (the journalist), his parents, his wife and his sister carp, cavil, harass, hector and finally attack one another with relentless trivia that detonate deeply buried resentments like emotional land mines . . . Moving past Broadway one-liners and easy gags, (Feiffer) makes laughter an adventure . . . This farce is Feiffer's exclusive specialty, and it's never been more harrowingly hilarious."—Newsweek. "Savagely funny."—N.Y. Times. "A compelling, devastating evening of theatre . . . the first adult play of the season."—Women's Wear Daily. (#9125)

LUNCH HOUR
(LITTLE THEATRE—COMEDY)
By JEAN KERR

3 men, 2 women—Interior

Never has Jean Kerr's wit had a keener edge or her comic sense more peaks of merriment than in this clever confection, starring Gilda Radner and Sam Waterston as a pair whose spouses are having an affair, and who have to counter by inventing an affair of their own. He, ironically, is a marriage counsellor, and a bit of a stick. His wife juggles husband, lover and mother and is a real go-getter. In fact, it was she who proposed to him. Of the other couple, the wife is a bit kooky. She can discourse on things tacky while wearing an evening gown with her jogging sneakers on; or, again, be overjoyed at the prospect of a trip to Paris: "And we'll never have to ask for french fried potatoes. They'll just come like that." While her husband, "Well, he's rich for a living." Or as he expresses it: "It's very difficult to do something if you don't need any money." All ends forgivingly for both couples, as the aggrieved wife concedes that they both "need something to regret," and the other husband concedes "I knew when I married that everyone would want to dance with you." "Civilized, charming, stylish . . . Very warm and most amusing . . . delicately interweaves laughter and romance."—N.Y. Times. "An amiable comedy about the eternal quadrangle . . . The author's most entertaining play in years."—N.Y. Daily News. "A beautiful weave of plot, character and laughs . . . It's delicious."—NBC-TV. (#674)